SONNY SAYS

Sorry!

CARYL HART

illustrated by **ZACHARIAH OHORA**

BLOOMSBURY
CHILDREN'S BOOKS

NEW YORK LONDON OXFORD NEW DELHI SYDNEY

It's a beautiful day.

Sonny and his friends are
playing hide-and-seek
when . . .

Ooh!

Sonny finds a box.

FOR: HONEY

Sonny really wants to know what's inside.
Sonny says,

A present?

First, Sonny pokes the box.

Sonny says,

Hello?

Sonny sniffs
the box.

Something smells
delicious.

Mmmm!

He forgets all about hide-and-seek until . . .

Sonny takes a
deep breath...

Then, very slowly,
he opens the box.

WOOF!

Boo and Sonny peek inside.

Inside the box is a huge chocolate cake,
covered in juicy, red strawberries!

Yummy!

says Boo.

Sonny gives Boo a strawberry.
Then he eats one too.

Now, Sonny wants a chocolate drop.
Sonny looks around . . .

Then he takes one
and eats it up.

Sonny says,

More!

Sonny takes ANOTHER
chocolate drop . . .

and ANOTHER!
Boo wants some too.

Sonny breaks off a BIG chunk of chocolate cake,
and they gobble it up quick-quick!

Sonny says,

Yummy!

Then they hear someone coming . . .

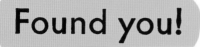

Found you!

says Honey.

Honey sees Sonny's chocolaty hands.
Honey sees Boo's chocolaty face.

Then Honey sees the open box . . .

Oh no! Honey starts to cry.

Sonny and Boo feel horrible.
What can they do?

Boo holds Honey's hand.

Sonny says,

Sorry!

But Honey doesn't stop crying.

Then Sonny has an idea . . .

Sonny says,

BAKE!

Sonny, Honey, and Boo bake
a new cake . . .

TOGETHER!

And it is . . .

Sonny says,

Come back soon!